Ka-chOWW!

By Ty Robinson
Illustrated by Todd Bright and Cristina Spagnoli
Designed by Tony Fejeran

Based on the characters and designs created by Pixar

Random House New York

ISBN: 978-0-7364-2531-5

www.randomhouse.com/kids/disney

Printed in the United States of America
10 9 8 7 6 5 4 3 2 1

"I am speed!" McQueen chanted as he focused on the dirt track stretched out in front of him. "Is my pit crew ready?"

"Standing by," said Luigi. "Tires ready!"

"Pit stop!" Guido added happily.

© Disney/Pixar

VAAA-ROOOOM! McQueen revved his engine—and took off!

"Woo-hooo!" he shouted. "It sure is great to zip around this dirt track after all that fancy stadium stuff. Out here, it's just me and—"

WHOOSH! "Whoa!" McQueen cried as he spun out of control. He was headed toward a cactus patch!

"I give you the best tires, but look—you still wipe out," Luigi remarked as he stared down at McQueen.

"Yeah, thanks," McQueen replied. "Ouch! My turns work perfectly on a real racetrack. Why can't I handle the dirt? I can't wait till my racing stadium is built. I'll be cruising then! Ka-ch**OWW!** Ow-ow-**OW!**"

"I told ya to steer right to go left. Can't you remember anything, hotshot?" It was Doc. He had been watching the whole time!

"Hey, Doc," replied McQueen. "What brings you out here, besides grumbling about my racing style?"

"That's exactly why I'm here!" Doc shouted back. "Mater, tow your rookie friend out of this mess!"

"Hey, buddy!" called Mater. "I'll have you outta there faster than a runaway tractor slidin' on an oil slick!"

Sure enough, Mater got him up and out of the patch in a jiffy.

"I'm going back to town," McQueen grumbled.

"Now, wait just a second, rookie!" Doc challenged McQueen. "If I'm crew chief, you gotta do things my way. Plus you're on my turf!"

"Whatever," McQueen said. "But first can I get cleaned up and take some of these prickles out of my tires? I think I scratched my paint job—"

"No!" interrupted Doc. "Try that turn again—unless it's too much for you, hotshot."

Reluctantly, McQueen stayed.

"New rules," lectured Doc. "No more worrying about your silly paint job. No more whining about a few cactus prickles. And no more rest until you make that turn look easy!"

McQueen tried the turn again . . .
and again . . . and again.

Sometimes he made it, and sometimes he didn't. "Ow-ow-OW!" he shouted each time he hit another cactus.

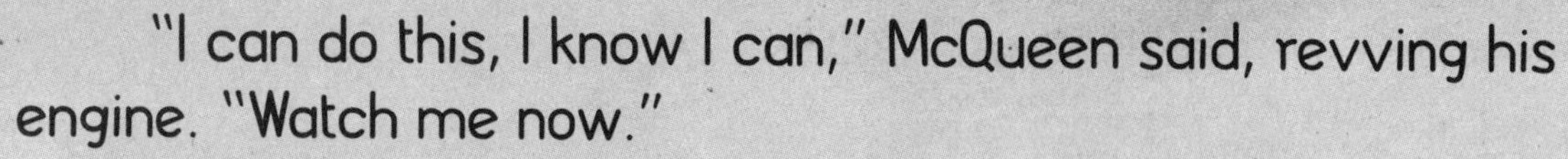

"I can do this, I know I can," McQueen said, revving his engine. "Watch me now."

Slowly, he returned to the starting line. Then, more determined than ever, he roared down the dirt track, concentrating on Doc's advice. And when he came to the curve, he glided around the corner—and stayed on the track!

"Ka-chow!" he hooted as he headed toward the finish line.

"Wahoo!" cried Mater. "You did it, buddy!"

"And with style!" added McQueen.

"Congratulations," said Doc. "You finally listened to some good advice."

"Yeah, the advice of a grumpy old car," McQueen spat back. Then he turned to Doc and grinned. "Feel like taking a little spin around the track?"

"Sure, rookie." Doc smiled and sped off. The race was on!